ADVENTURECAT
GOES TO SCHOOL

ADVENTURECAT GOES TO SCHOOL

by Susan Clymer

Illustrated by Kathy Rusynyk

A
LITTLE APPLE
PAPERBACK

SCHOLASTIC INC.
New York Toronto London Auckland Sydney

No part of this publication may be reproduced in whole or in part, or stored in a retrieval system, or transmitted in any form or by any means, electronic, mechanical, photocopying, recording, or otherwise, without written permission of the publisher. For information regarding permission, write to Scholastic Inc., Attention: Permissions Department,
555 Broadway, New York, NY 10012.

ISBN 0-590-37126-6

12 11 10 9 8 7 6 5 4
Printed in the U.S.A.
First Scholastic printing, September 1997

To independent spirits. . . .
Especially to Laula,
who touches my heart

ADVENTURECAT GOES TO SCHOOL

TALE'S BEGINNING

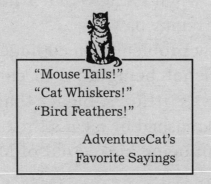

"Mouse Tails!"
"Cat Whiskers!"
"Bird Feathers!"

AdventureCat's
Favorite Sayings

I've had a nearly purrrrrrfect life since I decided to live with my human boy, Jesse. All fall long, I've swiped at his little sister's toes, and I've caught mice for his mother. I've sat in the windows and cleaned my fur to make myself shine. I've been a proper ruler of the house, a queenly cat.

But . . . Cat Whiskers!

Just when I'd gotten good at catching mice, the little tail-wigglers all moved out. Then, Pickles, the potbellied pig in the household, wasn't afraid of me anymore!

That's when I knew that I had a *cat*-astrophe on my paws.

My new problem seemed huge . . . bigger than not being able to catch mice when I was little . . . bigger than having my tail squashed by a car's tire . . . bigger even than being kicked out of MomCat's nest!

I, the AdventureCat, was *BORED*.

CHAPTER 1

"Every cat alive should be able to tell a good yowling story."

MomCat's Advice

More than anything, I wished I could talk to MomCat. She would understand.

My tail twitched as I sprang up on Jesse's windowsill. I still remembered every detail MomCat had taught me when I was a wobbly squirt. I remembered Brave Brother, Smart Sister, and Purry Brother and how we all lived together under the porch of that old farmhouse.

Jesse rolled over in bed. He always slept for hours during the very best part of the night. Humans just weren't adventurous enough for me! I looked outside at the tree branches waving in the wind. Perhaps I should go on a prowl tonight. Perhaps I should even move out into the meadow to be freeeee. I didn't need any sleepy boys. After all, I was an independent cat!

MomCat had explained to me that every cat should have a clean tail before going out to prowl. I started licking my tail. It had grown long enough so I could reach the crooked tip easily now.

White flakes began falling down from the sky. I stopped licking. Now this was something I'd never seen before! I watched as the ground turned white.

Jesse's window was open a little. I squeezed under and pushed on the screen. I was out! I leaped to my tree. I had to hold on tight to the branch. A white flake landed on my nose, so I growled. The white flake just disappeared! I skidded and scurried down the tree.

Then I pounced on the ground with my fiercest attack jump.

The ground was cold and wet! *"Yeeooooowww!"* My paws stung. I lifted as many feet as I could at one time. Then I lost my balance and fell forward onto my nose. The white flakes stuck all over my nose and whiskers. *"Ow! Meooww!"* Now my nose hurt.

This cold stuff was terrible!

I sunk my claws into the bark and zipped up the tree. I only skidded backward three times. I guess I still wasn't very good at climbing trees. I leaped for the window. Then I worked at the screen until I could slip back inside.

The warmest thing I could think of was Jesse. Desperately I hopped onto his back. He moaned when I landed on him, but I stretched out with my icy nose against his warm neck.

By morning, the white stuff covered the entire ground. It looked deeper than my belly. Mouse Tails! Was I stuck in this house just when I needed to get out and see the world?

Jesse jumped out of bed. Usually it took him a lot longer to get up in the mornings. "Snow!" he yelled at the top of his lungs.

I headed downstairs to check the windows on the other side of the house. Was the white stuff there, too? I saw Pickles asleep in a tight ball by the radiator and swatted at her as I went by. The pig didn't even bother to move.

I prowled through the house, rowling. How in catnip was I going to go on an adventure now? This stuff called snow seemed to be everywhere. I marched into the kitchen.

"Hi, Kittencat." Jesse's mom patted my head.

Kittencat? What an undignified name! "Try Meeeooowwwser," I sang.

Jesse slid into the kitchen on his stocking feet. His hair stuck straight up.

"Your birthday is coming this Friday," Mom said, handing Jesse the milk carton as he skidded past. "Is there anything special you want for a present?"

Jesse slid into his chair. "How about a new sled?" He poured milk on his cereal and took a bite. "Hey, I'm the Special Student in my class this week since it's my birthday! That means I get to take something for Show-and-Tell every day."

Jesse's little sister, Anna, stomped into

the room, squeezing her stuffed cat upside down in her arms.

My skin shivered. I hoped she never squeezed me that way! I leaped onto the windowsill by Jesse's place at the table. Snow was out there, too! I howled at the white stuff, completely fed up.

Jesse's mom put her hands over her ears. "What's gotten into that kitten?"

I felt so desperate that I wailed deep in my throat, then soared into a high-pitched cry.

"Be quiet, Wildcat!" Jesse exclaimed.

I flattened my ears at Jesse. Had everybody forgotten who was the boss around here?

CHAPTER 2

"Children and dogsss
have no dignity."

from *Cat Proverbs*

Jesse carried me upstairs with one arm around my belly. He let my legs hang. "Oh, Wildcat," he said, "when are you going to learn not to make Mom mad?" In the doorway to our room, he suddenly clutched me tighter. "I know what I'll do with you!"

I tried to break loose. Young humans are dangerous when they talk like that. Before I could get free, Jesse stuffed me into a box and closed the door. The last time I'd been in that box, he'd taken me to a cat party at a shopping mall!

I yowled and pushed my head against the bars of the door!

Jesse hummed to himself. Then he carried my box outside. The air was cold. I stuck my paw out one of the holes and tried my best to snag his fingers. "Let me outttt, foolish booooyyyy!"

"You wanted to go on an adventure, didn't you?" Jesse replied, laughing.

Startled, I stopped right in the middle of a good screech. MomCat had told me that only cats could read minds. Was my Jesse getting smarter?

Jesse set my carrier down on a long flat thing that looked a little like a box with low sides. Then the entire thingamajig began to move. It slid along the snow! What in *cat*-lamity was happening to me now? I bounced along inside my carrier.

Then Jesse hopped on behind me, and we went sailing down a hill. I just hoped I

didn't fall off into that white stuff. We flew faster than even MomCat could run!

Jesse cheered, and I sang right along with him.

When we came to a stop, I heard children's voices. Lots of children milled around us. I hunkered down, silent and small. I hoped they weren't in that squeezing stage, like Anna.

Where were we?!

Jesse lifted up my carrier again and held it tightly against his chest. "Don't worry, Wildcat," he murmured as he pulled the slider over and leaned it against the wall. Jesse stepped inside a building. Now the noise was louder than all the cats in the neighborhood when they get together for a full-moon meeting!

Jesse ran. I couldn't see where we were going at all. "Mrs. Whitehorse!" Jesse stopped so fast that I thumped against the end of the carrier. "I brought my cat for Show-and-Tell."

A woman peered through the bars at me. She had strange round things in front of her eyes that made her eyes look big. I growled low in my throat.

"See, she's purring," Jesse said.

That foolish woman believed him. "Jesse, did you forget my rule?" she asked. "You're only allowed to bring a pet to class with a parent's help." I barely resisted snagging some of her long wiggly hair.

"Oh," Jesse replied, disappointed.

Mrs. Whitehorse patted his arm. "Why don't you put the carrier on your desk while I make the morning announcements?"

Other children ran into the room and surrounded me. They sounded just like excited dogs . . . rambunctious dogs. I made every hair on my body stand on end so that I looked *gigantic*. A piercing bell rang, and the group of children left.

"Isn't this exciting?" Jesse whispered to

me. "How many cats ever get to go to school? I hope the teacher lets you stay a while."

School? So this was the place Jesse went each day.

While Mrs. Whitehorse spoke, I chewed on the fur between my claws. What in mouse tails did all the children do here every day? Then I heard the teacher call my human's name. "Jesse! Since you're our Special Student this week, I've decided you can go ahead and show your kitten. We'll call your mother afterward to come take it home."

Had that lady just called me an *it*? Besides, I was a cat, not a kitten!

Too much had happened to me this morning. The moment Jesse opened my box, I set all my claws into his hands, and I climbed.

"Ow, ow, ow!" Jesse exclaimed.

He couldn't keep hold of me. I leaped for the top of a bookcase. Then I sat and looked down. It was a grand sight. Mrs.

Whitehorse had her hand over her mouth. The children sat frozen. I gave my paw one lick and straightened my whiskers. I had to admit, this wasn't boring like home.

All at once, everybody screamed. Jesse jumped at me and tried to catch my *tail*! Three girls raced up to the bookcase, their grabby hands outstretched.

The fur on my tail fluffed out in shock. I had no choice. I sailed from the top of the bookcase onto the desk in front of Mrs. Whitehorse. I landed on a piece of paper and slid. A plant on the corner went flying. A framed picture crashed down. The teacher reached for me.

I leaped again. I landed on the windowsill. Then I saw the perfect place to get out of reach. Way up high, there was a kind of branch coming out from the wall. A piece of cloth hung down from the branch. But it was a *long* way up. I sprang straight upward and landed on the branch. I'd made it! Bird Feathers, I really was getting big!

"Get off the flag!" Jesse yelled, standing beneath me.

I felt proud of myself. Not very many cats could have balanced on such a little branch. "Not on your one liffffffee!" I hissed.

CHAPTER 3

"Look at me,
I'm a mascot!"

from *AdventureCat's
School Song*

I, the AdventureCat, watched the children stroll out of the room, one by one. "Let's give the kitten a chance to calm down while we go to music," Mrs. Whitehorse said.

Jesse was the last child in line. He glared up at me. Then the teacher closed the door firmly.

I was alone. My feet did ache a bit, and I was getting awfully wobbly from balancing on that skinny little branch. I bounded down and landed with a jarring thump. I needed to work on my landings. Then I stalked the room, my tail held high.

So this was school! I hopped onto Jesse's desk and tapped his pencil. It was fun to watch the pencil roll down the desk and then fall off. Next, I saw a little tree by Mrs. Whitehorse's desk. My claws itched to be sharpened. Just as I was scratching the tree, a sweet scent tickled my nose.

I crouched down and waited. A mouse raced along the floorboards. On only my third pounce, I caught the mouse's tail with my claws. Ah, but I was a great hunter now.

I ate only the tasty bottom of the mouse, just like MomCat had taught me. I was cleaning my whiskers after my meal when the door opened. The teacher peered inside. She gasped. "Come in quietly, class."

I picked up my mouse head and leaped onto Jesse's desk. None of those children was going to take it away from me!

This time the children bumped into one another to get away from me. One girl even screeched. A boy squeezed his eyes shut. He looked like a sick kitten. Didn't human children know a good lunch when they saw one? Jesse sat down with a *thunk* and rolled his eyes at me. I rubbed my head against his chin in greeting.

Mrs. Whitehorse walked closer. To my surprise, she scratched my head with two fingers. "Good kitty." I dropped my mouse head, and she whisked it up in a paper towel.

Thief!! I meowed. Thief!

The teacher buried my prize in the trash. Then she asked a child to take the trash out of the room. Next, she said, "Jesse, would you mind if Wildcat stayed with us for this week? She could be our official class mascot."

Jesse didn't answer. He cocked his head sideways at me.

The lady scratched me harder. "I'm certain the principal wouldn't mind. The

school does have a bit of a mouse problem."

"I'd miss you at home, Wildcat," Jesse
murmured to me, "but I'd get to see you
here every day." He glanced up at the
teacher and said, "I guess she can stay."

He hadn't even asked me!

Well, I'd wanted an adventure. Besides,
Mrs. Whitehorse was turning out to be an
awfully good head-scratcher. I wasn't sure

what "official class mascot" meant, but it sounded important. MomCat had told me that people sometimes make statues of important cats and dogs. I leaned into the woman's hand. I could imagine a statue of the AdventureCat under the flag. My eyes even began to close. I kept one open a slit. After all, cats have to be ready for anything.

The teacher stopped scratching and looked at me oddly. She tilted her head. Then she swung her eyepieces on a string around her neck. "Perhaps we'd better not feed the cat. She'll be more likely to catch mice if she's good and hungry."

My eyes popped open wide. I couldn't believe my ears.

"Not feed her?!" Jesse cried, rising to his feet. Then he added hesitantly, "Well, ma'am, if you really think that's best."

I sat up as straight as a tree trunk. What was this Mrs. Whitehorse . . . a secret enemy of all cats?

CHAPTER 4

"Remember, my kittens —
curiosity CAN kill a cat."

MomCat's Warning

I stretched out on Jesse's lap to claim him . . . just in case these human youngsters didn't understand that he was *mine*. I draped my head across his arm all day, so he had trouble drawing with his pencil. I ignored everyone else, especially Mrs. Whitehorse. I didn't trust her. Maybe I should think of her as Mrs. White-*dog*.

When Jesse put on his jacket in the afternoon, I jumped onto his shoulder. Then I scrambled down inside the front of his jacket to let him know I wanted to go home.

Jesse tugged me out tail end first in a very undignified way. "You *like* catching mice, Wildcat. You'll have a fine time." Yet he sounded worried. Jesse set me down on his desk.

"Happy hunting!" Mrs. Whitehorse called cheerfully. Then Jesse and Mrs. Whitehorse left the room together!

I was all alone, without any food. I had only water. Worse than that, I had no idea what might happen at a school at night. What if dogs came visiting . . . or gangs of wide-eyed raccoons? MomCat had told me about raccoons.

I tried to open the door. I had to leap up at the round knob. It slipped through my paws.

Out of the corner of my eye, I saw something hop at the back of the room. My back end wiggled, despite myself. That creature must have been waiting for the children to leave before coming out. I fearlessly bounded half the length of the room and pounced. I missed, but I sure scared that beetle.

Suddenly the door opened. *Creeaaakkk*. I bounded onto the bookcase. The lights blinked on. I sat up there with my front paws draped over the edge, and my tail wrapped around my feet. I held myself very still. A man began to sweep the floor with a big broom that sent up lovely dust balls.

Now, I'd never really met a grown human man . . . only females, like Jesse's mom and Mrs. Whitehorse. My ear tips tickled with curiosity.

The man worked his way around the room until he stood beneath me. His hair looked delightfully fluffy. It even bounced a little as he swept.

The man leaned down to pick up a pencil. All of his hair slipped sideways on his head! I'd never seen that happen before. Did grown boys have hair that moved around on their heads?

The man pushed his hair back in place with one hand as he stood up. His head was now directly beneath me. I couldn't resist. I leaned down and hooked his hair with one claw. Then I lifted gently. His hair came right off his head and dangled on the end of my claw. I swung the hair back and forth.

The man reached up to touch his bare head. *"What on earth?"* he cried, twisting to look up at me. His eyes got as round as chicken eggs. He blinked.

I rowled at him, just a friendly hello. Then I waved his hair so he could see it was safe.

The man blinked again. He snatched his hair out of my grasp and exclaimed, "A bobcat at school?!"

Naturally I narrowed my eyes and hissed back at him.

He stuffed his hair into his shirt pocket. Then he shook his broom right at me. Was he dangerous? I stretched out my claws and swiped at him, using three quick *waps* the way MomCat had taught me. The man backed out of the room. "There's nothing I hate more than cats!" he yelled, as the lights went off. He slammed the door so hard that the windows shook.

Flying fur! He was loud. I flattened my ears. Did all grown-up boys make this much noise?

I started washing myself from my tip to my tail. Then again, the man had thought I was a bobcat. I licked my paw and rubbed one ear. Bobcats were my fiercest cousins. That human had seen my true worth.

I didn't stop cleaning until darkness filled the room. Then I peered around. Jesse always fed me at night. My stomach ached! I hopped off the bookcase and landed on my boy's desk. *"Meeoooowwwww,"* I howled. "Let me ouuuuuttttttt!" I had the kitty jitters.

I yowled, long drawn-out screeches. I hated being shut in a strange place. So, I did the only thing a reasonable cat could do. I crawled inside Jesse's desk. It was a tight fit. Books crashed to the floor. His pencils rolled out. I curled up in a ball on Jesse's papers and kept watch late into the night.

CHAPTER 5

"Stalk those moths,
Roll that mouse!"

from *A Kitten's Melody*

When Jesse came to school the next
morning, I just let him call for me. Soon,
he peered into his desk.

"There you are, Wildcat." He stroked me
between my eyes. "What did you do to the
janitor? There's a sign on the door that
says DANGEROUS CAT! ENTER AT YOUR OWN
RISK."

Jesse had food smell on his hands. I
scrambled out. A container on his desk

smelled so good that my tail sprang straight up in the air.

"Those are the class treats for my birthday," Jesse whispered to me. "You get one, just like everybody else. I brought your favorite, cheese balls."

"Ooooopen uup!" I rowled. Everyone laughed.

"Since your treats are healthy, Jesse, you may pass them out while I'm doing the announcements," Mrs. Whitehorse said. "Once the food is gone, maybe the kitten will settle down." The teacher pointed her glasses at me. "Just make sure you don't feed her. She didn't catch one mouse last night!"

I turned away from her. She didn't need to rub it in. Besides, Mrs. White-*wolf* hadn't caught any mice, either.

Jesse handed out the first three treats to the children in the back row. I followed him. When the teacher was reading, he dropped the fourth one on the floor. I've never gobbled up a cheese ball so fast. Next, the girl in pigtails invited me onto her lap and sneaked me hers. Such a nice girl, I thought. She knew that cats should come first.

My stomach finally stopped grumbling.

I was ready for *this* day's school adventure. So, I sat up tall on Jesse's desk. "Hey, look!" Jesse said to me, tapping a new piece of paper taped to his desk. "Mrs. Whitehorse gave you a name tag, too."

"Geography time!" Mrs. Whitehorse announced. She picked up a long stick and pointed to a picture on the wall. I decided I might as well help. I waved my back end from side to side and pounced on Mrs. Whitehorse's stick when the tip touched the desk.

The children giggled. I got carried away and chased my tail in the front of the room. Even Mrs. Whitehorse laughed. Laughing must be important at school. Perhaps that was the reason children came to school!

I strolled back to Jesse's desk using my best swagger. I imagined I looked like a bobcat. I even puffed out my cheeks. That made my whiskers spring out wide.

Now every child pulled a book out of his desk and started to read. I sat on Jesse's book and cleaned a back foot. "Silly cat," Jesse whispered and shooed me off. He dragged one finger across the page, muttering to himself. He moved his finger faster. I couldn't resist. I batted at his hand, then grabbed his finger in my teeth. I knew enough not to really bite.

This was a game cats understood. It was almost as good a game as when Jesse wiggled his toes under the covers at home.

Suddenly a little notion wiggled in my mind, and I figured out even more.

Children didn't come to school only to laugh. Why, I wasn't just an AdventureCat. I must be a CleverCat! I wished I could tell Smart Sister, Brave Brother, and Purry Brother. I had solved the mystery of school! It was as obvious as my whiskers. Children came to school to learn how to play games! Every day, children learned how to point sticks and draw with pencils, walk in lines, eat tasty treats, and talk to flags.

CHAPTER 6

"In the greatest age, humans worshipped cats as gods and goddesses."

from *Cat History*, passed on from every mother to her kittens

Moonlight always made me frisky. I stayed alert that night. I stalked! I pounced! And I caught two *scrawny* mice. I liked *fat, plump, chubby* mice. Still, the little tweakers kept me from starving. I left their heads on Mrs. White-*frog's* chair. When I heard voices the next morning, I leaped onto the flagpole. I barely made it.

Sure enough, the teacher came in first. She dropped an armload of papers on her desk. Then she sat right on the mice.

With a strangled gasp, Mrs. Whitehorse leaped to her feet. "Wildcat!" she yelled.

I meowed at her in my sweetest voice.

Mrs. Whitehorse didn't even give me a reward! Every time I caught a mouse at home, Jesse's mom gave me a bowl of milk. All this teacher did was to give me two stars on my name tag!

Mrs. Whitehorse was a true villain.

I stayed up there on the flag. The students said the pledge of allegiance to me that morning. I bowed my ears graciously. I wanted them to have a fine image of me as the mascot — for my statue.

I had figured out why these children came to school, but I still couldn't understand why Mrs. Whitehorse was here. Most of all, I couldn't understand why all the children seemed to like her so much.

Why would they like someone who starved cats?!

Jesse walked to the front of the room. He grinned up at me, then faced his class. "For my Show-and-Tell this morning, I brought in five minutes of my favorite rock music." He punched a button on a machine.

My hair stood up on end! That music sounded like car horns blaring, children screaming, even cats fighting! Yet Jesse snapped his fingers and wiggled his shoulders. Other children clapped their hands.

"Turn it way down," Mrs. Whitehorse called.

I noticed the door open a crack. I hopped down from the flag and slipped away. I padded down the hall like a lion. I, the AdventureCat, was freeeeeee. I passed rooms full of children. I was proud to be an independent cat. I trotted down some steps.

Suddenly I smelled food, glorious *food*. I couldn't help myself. I zipped into a room full of clanking pans and talking humans. I danced around the legs until I found the most mouth-watering smells. I looked up at a grown human male. Uh-oh. I'd better make this robbery fast. I leaped onto the counter and snagged a piece of chicken bird.

"My, my! What have we here?" a voice asked.

He didn't sound dangerous . . . or loud. Still, I growled and hunched over my catch. The man in the tall hat began *singing* to me,

"A kitty at school!
Who looks ready for a duel."

I peered at him sideways as I chewed. Everybody knew that *cats* were usually the best singers in the world.

The man waved his giant spoon at me, and his voice soared higher,

"What do you take me for . . . a fool?
Don't worry, cat, I'm cool."

And he flipped me another piece of chicken bird.

Now this just might be the ideal human.

I gobbled up his gift. The man had the roundest belly I'd ever seen. It wiggled when he sang. He kept singing a cat opera about beautiful and brave cats. And he kept tossing me bits of chicken bird. When I felt ready to pop, he gently picked me up and carried me back out into the hallway.

I squeezed my eyes at him in farewell. Then I padded away. When I got back to Jesse's room, I sprang onto Mrs. Whitehorse's desk.

"You're back!" she exclaimed. "Where have you been?" I stretched myself out so she could see my fat round belly. I had outwitted the villain. Her mouth fell open.

"Chicken birrrrrrdddddd," I purred proudly.

CHAPTER 7

> "For four long hungry nights, I dreamed of
>   Catching fat mice
>   Gobbling chicken bird
>   Munching cheese balls
>   . . . Even chewing cookie dough."
>
> from *AdventureCat's School Song*

My whiskers twitched and then twitched again as I awakened the next morning. I opened one eye a slit and peered at the room from my nest on the teacher's desk. No human seemed ready to pounce on me. No big dog was slobbering to eat me.

Still, something was wrong. I could feel it in my whiskers! My whiskers always told me the truth. I looked around the room, with the familiar desks and the plants. Suddenly I understood. Being bored at home had been a bother. Having no regular meals here was horrible. But being trapped in this school was an insult. And all cats *hate* insults.

It was time to escape.

Jesse brought in his colored sticks and a picture for his fourth day of Show-and-Tell. He seemed proud to have me in front of the class with him. I, on the other paw, had had enough of this adventure! I walked across his feet, then rubbed against his legs to let him know I needed to talk. He just smiled at me, showing his teeth in that odd way humans do.

"Keyboarding time for Group A," Mrs. Whitehorse announced. "Everyone else please work on your globes."

Jesse moved to a seat in front of one of those mysterious boxes in the back of the room. I perched right on top of Jesse's box. That way I could get his attention. A light flashed, and the box beeped! I sprang straight up into the air. Then I crept forward to stare over the top of the box. Figures zipped across the screen. I couldn't resist trying to nab one. This was a good catly game.

Still, I might not find a better time for my private talk with Jesse. I hopped onto his shoulder. He leaned his head against mine. "Even Mom misses you, Computer Cat."

"Mrow!" I cried miserably. "I'm starving." I climbed down his arm to his wrist. His fingers kept moving, pushing buttons. "Get me ouuuutttt of herrrrre," I meowed.

"You're right, Wildcat!" my human replied. "School *is* fun." Jesse kissed me on the top of the head. Then he scooped me up under my belly and dropped me on the ground. "I have to practice typing, Wildcat. I'll play with you later."

Bird Feathers! I had thought Jesse was getting smarter at reading minds . . . but today he couldn't even understand a few perfectly clear words!

Maybe I'd just go visit the singing man

with the big belly. At that thought, I froze with one paw in the air. Why, I'd bet a plump mouse that Jesse and his mom would like the cook as much as I did! Perhaps the man could cook chicken bird and sing in *our* kitchen! I'd go ask him right now if he wanted to come home with me. Then Jesse could take us both home on his snow-sliding thingamajig.

I surveyed the room. I needed to be very, very clever right now. Good! The girl with the longest hair was heading for the door. She had her globe clasped under one arm. I belly-walked beside her, not making a single sound.

Before I even got to the door, Mrs. Whitehorse swooped down on me. "I'm keeping an eagle eye out for vanishing kitties today!" She laughed and set me down on Jesse's desk.

I cleaned the white patch on my chest furiously.

But *cats* never give up.

When Mrs. Whitehorse called, "Gym!" I

lined up behind Jesse. The pigtailed girl came next. Neither of the children gave me away. They didn't even look at me. I held my head and tail high. Just as I strolled through the doorway, old Mrs. White-*eagle* snatched me up in her arms.

I hissed at her, but she stroked me from my ears to my tail. Cat Whiskers! That woman was a good back-scratcher!

In the afternoon, I paced back and forth across the window ledge by my water bowl. If I didn't get out of here, I'd become as nutty as a *chipmunk*! That was a horrible thought! I sprang from the bookcase to the window ledge, over and over again.

White flakes started coming down out of the sky. More snow! This time, the white stuff blew sideways.

A woman with a bow in her hair pushed a cart into the room. I stopped pacing to watch the paper fluttering on the cart. A few ribbons hung off the edge.

"Yippee!" Jesse called. "Art!"

What did "art" mean?

Mrs. Whitehorse left the room. The woman with the bow in her hair handed out a big sheet of paper to every student. She also gave each of them a bottle. Next, she handed out sheets of crinkly paper, and the students started ripping these up into little squares.

I pounced on one boy's desk and tried to knock his squares off. I stuck my paw up over the edge of Jesse's desk and stole a bunch of his.

"Give those back!" Jesse exclaimed in his fed-up voice. "They're for my mosaic."

I hesitated. Maybe I was playing the game wrong. Then the pigtailed girl started squeezing little drops out of her bottle. I leaped onto her desk and batted at one. Only the drop didn't go flying like water does in the sink. The drop stuck to my paw!

I licked my paw. Oooohh. I had to hold my tongue out in the air because of the terrible taste. I set my paw down in the middle of the girl's squares. Three of them stuck to my paw. I stood up and shook my paw. The squares wouldn't come off!

The girl giggled. "Stay still, and I'll help, Wildcat."

I hopped backward. I bounded right through the globs of sticky stuff and skidded over her squares of paper. Now I had paper stuck to every foot! How undignified! I shook my feet harder, two at a time.

"Wildcat's dancing!" Jesse yelled. Everyone laughed, even the lady with the bow in her hair.

I narrowed my eyes at Jesse, still shaking two legs. I flattened my ears and yowled. This was not funny. In fact, this was a true *cat*-lamity!

"She's square dancing," Jesse howled.

Now . . . even my own human had turned against me!

CHAPTER 8

"Remember your dignity!
Cuddle, but never ever
drool."

from *A Kitten's Melody*

I was determined to win my freeeeee-
dom now. The battle had begun. It was me
against this whole school. I waited by the
door as if it were a mouse hole. The man
Jesse called the janitor hadn't been there
for two nights. Still, cats are good at waiting, especially me. My stomach ached with
hunger. As the sun set, I heard footsteps
coming down the hall. The steps stopped
outside the door. I crouched, ready.

The doorknob twisted, and the janitor tiptoed into the room. I dashed between his legs and out into the hallway.

"Fool cat!" he yelled.

My tail flew out behind me, I ran so fast. I raced past closed classroom doors and down to the end of the hall.

The man chased me into a big room. Ropes hung down from the high ceiling. I streaked straight up one of the ropes. I perched on a knot. "Can't catch meeeeee," I sang. The man waved his arms. Then he stomped out, his hair crooked on his head.

That's when I noticed I was as high as the roof of a house! I had to climb down that rope *backward*. My heart began pounding in my kitty chest. Halfway down, the rope started swinging. *Yeoww!* I dug my claws in as I sailed back and forth.

I swung faster and faster. I sailed farther and farther.

Actually, this was fun! I slithered down

to sit safely on another knot. Then I swayed across the room, over and over again.

My stomach gurgled at me. No matter how exciting this might be, I had to hunt for food. I bounded to the ground and set off to find the singing cook. He wasn't in his den. So, I stalked the lower hall looking for mice. I was hungry enough to eat ten little tail-wigglers.

To my surprise, I came to a door that I knew how to open. I leaped up and pulled down on the flat latch with my front paws. I heard a satisfying *CLICK*. The door swung open.

This room looked different than the others at school. Best of all, there were lots of cubbyholes for hiding. I heard another *CLICK* behind me. The door had shut! Still, I smelled a tempting odor. I belly-walked past child-sized paper dolls. I crept around piles of blocks.

Something furry moved in the corner!

Instantly the tip of my tail wiggled. So did my ears. Yet I didn't make a sound.

I chose an air attack. I sprang up, my ears flat and my paws close to my body. As I sailed, I saw my prey clearly . . . a rabbit, as big as me! Cat Whiskers! This could be a feast!! I extended all my sharp claws. I was so pleased that I chattered deep in my throat. The rabbit hopped, and I came down . . . onto the rug.

My claws stuck into the rug. I pulled them out and galloped after the fluffy creature. MomCat had taught me that cats could catch rabbits. The rabbit made a sharp turn, and I tore right past him. What MomCat hadn't taught me was that rabbits have a few tricks of their own.

I stopped, panting. Then I carefully stalked that rabbit. I didn't let kitty excitement take me over again. I crept as quietly as a cat in a chicken coop. I pounced. I batted. With a final great leap, I landed solidly on the rabbit's back! I opened my mouth to bite. Ah, dinner! The bunny shook beneath me with terror.

I, the AdventureCat, was a mighty hunter.

I lowered my mouth onto its fur. Instead of biting, I found myself licking the animal's neck! The rabbit didn't try to run. It didn't even wiggle beneath me. The bunny just panted. Maybe it was young, like me.

The creature had a shockingly dirty head. I licked the rabbit's forehead and wrapped my paws around its neck. I'd eat it later. I'd win my freedom later, too. Right now, this rabbit seemed as cuddly as I remembered my brothers and sister being when we were wobbly squirts. I hadn't enjoyed this feeling in so long. The rabbit felt as warm as MomCat!

I fell asleep, purring so hard that I drooled.

CHAPTER 9

"Cats of the world!
What animal hops high?
Zigzags like a champ?
Tastes good?
Is warm and cuddly?
Yet bewitches with his soft eyes?
Can you guess?"

AdventureCat's Riddle

A woman with white hair stared at me, her face close. She clearly didn't believe what she was seeing. "Hopper?" she whispered. She had deep lines in her skin. Then the strange woman saw that I was awake. To my surprise, she squeezed her eyes respectfully at me in greeting.

Most humans don't understand cat sign language. I yawned back politely. She reached out with one finger and touched the animal in my paws.

In my paws?! Mouse Feathers! I mean, Bird Tails! What was I doing lying on top of a rabbit?

Then I remembered last night. I had promised myself I would eat this bunny later. Well, I was starving this very moment! I squeezed my prey. The rabbit opened its eyes and looked fondly at me.

"You're fine, Hopper. Thank goodness!" the lady said.

The rabbit's dark eyes were soft with trust. Oh, I didn't want to eat him. Not now. Not ever. Somehow, he had become a friend. The rabbit leaned his head closer and touched his wiggling nose to mine. He was making sounds, but I didn't understand his language. I just felt like purring.

"I've never seen anything like this in my life," the woman said. "You must be Mrs. Whitehorse's new class mascot, you wonderful cat." I rolled over on my back so she could scratch my stomach. "What are you doing here in my kindergarten room?" I watched as the woman took a pencil and a pad of paper out of a pocket in her skirt and began to draw.

Why, she was drawing me! Maybe she would be the one who would make my statue, too. She must be a teacher, too, just like Mrs. Whitehorse.

The piercing bell rang. Children ran into the room. They weren't big like Jesse. These were smaller monsters. The children raced, squealing, right at me.

One boy was about to pounce on me. I recognized the attack look in his eyes. I hunched beside the bunny in horror. Hopper sat up on his back feet and raised his ears straight up. But the teacher put out her hand. That's all she did. And the boy stopped running! He stopped squealing! I couldn't believe it. A whole classroom of children not much bigger than Anna, and not one of them tried to pull my tail or squish me.

It was all because of the teacher. I was sure of it. Hopper stretched back out on the floor. The children sat down and folded their grabby hands in their laps. Mouse Tails and Bird Feathers! Maybe this was what grown-ups did in classrooms. They kept the children from being tail-pullers. The children played games all day, and the teachers stopped the biters and the eye-scratchers. Just like MomCat used to do!

I purred and kneaded the soft rabbit's back. The rabbit scooted around so that his head rested against my side. I wanted to drool, that furry rabbit felt so good. But it was undignified to drool in front of all those people.

"Good morning, class," the teacher said.

"Good morning, Ms. Wells," the children answered all together.

"As you see, our pet Hopper has a new friend," Ms. Wells said. Then she added, "Welcome to Friday, children."

I stopped kneading for a second and raised my head. Friday? Jesse's mom had said that Friday was Jesse's birthday! I wasn't certain what a birthday meant, but I knew it was important. Then I had a horrible thought. Perhaps this was the time when Jesse's mom would kick him out of the nest like MomCat had done to me!

I gave the rabbit's head one last lick in farewell. I hoped I would see him again, but Jesse was my most important friend, even if he had laughed at me in Art. Then I stood and ran to the door. "Ooooopen up!" I rowled.

That wonderful Ms. Wells held the door open wide! I rubbed against her legs to say, "Thank you." Then I padded down the hallway and up the stairs toward Jesse's classroom.

No matter what, I had to go back to Jesse. He would need his cat on his birthday.

CHAPTER 10

"If persuading doesn't work,
If dignity fails,
Try creating a ruckus."

from *Cat Proverbs*

I hadn't eaten a bite in two days. I must have looked as skinny as a whisker. Still, I strolled into the classroom with my best bobcat walk.

"Wildcat!" Jesse bounded out of his seat. He picked me up and hugged me. Oh, Cat Whiskers and Bird Feathers! Jesse did care about me! I licked his cheek, then purred about his birthday.

Mrs. Whitehorse pointed at me with her

finger. "*You* certainly sent the janitor into an uproar last night!"

"Whoo meee?" I rowled in as pleasant a way as I could manage. After all, Jesse liked her. Then I remembered what I had figured out about teachers. But humans Jesse's size didn't need to be told not to pull tails, did they? Still, the youngsters could get rambunctious. Mrs. Whitehorse must be here to keep the peace, too.

I butted at Jesse's chin, pleased with myself for figuring out the mystery of school. I wished I could talk to MomCat. She had been right . . . cats were much smarter than humans. Why, I had seen children at school almost as small as Anna and lots bigger than Jesse. Children had to go to school almost forever. We cats only had to live with MomCat for six weeks to learn what we needed to know to be properly behaved.

Just then, Jesse's mom walked in the doorway. "What are you doing heeerrrreeee?" I asked, amazed to see her.

Why, Jesse must be bringing his mother for Show-and-Tell today!

Jesse's mom tugged at a rope. To my astonishment, she dragged Pickles into the classroom! The potbellied pig held her stiff legs straight out in front of her. What was that pig doing here? I was the only mascot this class needed!

"Pickles!" Jesse cried. And he *dropped* me.

Why in fur balls would he drop me for a pig? Of course, I landed on my paws. "Squarehead," I hissed at Pickles.

Jesse gave Pickles a giant hug. "This is my potbellied pig!" he exclaimed to the class.

Those kids acted more excited than when I had arrived. Even the girl in pigtails squealed, "She's so cute!"

"I named her Pickles after my favorite food," Jesse added. "Pickles is as smart as a dog and very clean."

Dogs weren't smart! And I was cleaner than that pig. How foolish could Jesse get?

"Ugly round nose," I meowed.

Jesse didn't notice, but the pig snorted. Pickles looked right at me as I rubbed up against Jesse's leg. Jesse pushed me aside with his foot. "Not now, Wildcat!"

I had come back here to be with Jesse just because it was his birthday. I was starving. And now this rotten pig was in *my* classroom, trying to take over *my* boy. I swatted at Pickle's nose. "Oaf. Monster."

Her snorting escalated into loud angry squeals. Children covered their ears. I flattened my own ears and rowled loudly, "Dirty pig."

That last insult got her. I knew it would. She hated being called dirty. The pig lunged forward. Jesse never could hold her when she got really upset. The leash jerked out of his hands.

I jumped up on Jesse's desk, and the pig chased me. I raced around the room. Pickles whacked into the tree by the teacher's desk. The tree fell over with a

62

crash. Pickles knocked against the trash can with her side, and it rolled across the room. Papers and Kleenex went flying. I danced along the windowsill. I liked this game. Pickles barreled right through the students' globes to try to get at me. Every one of the globes wobbled and then bounced across the floor.

Children began to scream. They raced everywhere, grabbing for their globes.

I jumped up on the flagpole. The pig still ran in circles. She hadn't figured out where I had gone. Jesse and his mom raced after Pickles. Jesse was within a hand's length of grabbing the pig.

"Wildcat!" Mrs. Whitehorse shrieked. "Look what you've done!"

I had to admit that it was a wonderful sight.

Pickles pulled her tail out of Jesse's fingers and lumbered into the hallway. She skittered out of sight.

Jesse's mom's face fell. "Oh, my good-ness."

"*Now* we have a problem," Mrs. White-horse said.

Jesse skidded out the door. I jumped down and gave chase, too. The whole class followed me, as loud as twenty excited Dalmatians. "Hush, children," Mrs. White-horse called. Kids in other rooms started popping their heads out of doorways. Soon we had a whole gang rushing down the hall.

Mrs. Whitehorse glared at me as she rushed past. I knew I had finally paid Mrs. White-*snake* back for starving me.

Pickles skittered into the large room with the swinging ropes. Jesse and his mom and Mrs. Whitehorse and I entered together. With a flying leap, Jesse caught Pickles around the belly. The pig was so upset I thought she was going to bite him for a second. Jesse's mom grabbed the leash and held on tight.

The instant Jesse stood up, I jumped onto his shoulder to claim him.

"There's Hopper's friend!" a voice

yelled. The class of the smallest humans were bouncing balls in the corner.

I meowed in recognition. I even rowled at Mrs. White-*snail* to show her I didn't hold any grudge.

"Oh, Wildcat," Jesse exclaimed, and his voice cracked.

My Jesse was scared? I leaned my head against his cheek. I'd been right. Jesse did need me on his birthday.

"Why are these children out of their classrooms?" a man's voice asked. Then the voice rose, "What is a PIG doing in the gym?"

Jesse gasped, "The principal!"

I froze in mid-purr. What in flying bird feathers was a "principal"? Every person in the room fell completely silent. Pickles kept right on snorting. Jesse's mom put her arm around Jesse from behind, and she patted me.

A man came closer to Jesse and me. He didn't have any hair on his head at all. In fact, the top of his head looked like a shiny ball. This must be the principal!

Mrs. Whitehorse stepped back, as if he were the head cat in a neighborhood.

The principal pointed at the snorting pig. "I am going to make a new rule!" he exclaimed. "No large pets may visit this school. That means *no pigs allowed*!!" The bump in his throat went up and down as he swallowed.

The principal gazed at Mrs. Whitehorse. The teacher shrugged, her cheeks pale. Mouse Tails! Didn't that foolish man know that it wasn't the teacher's fault that Pickles had gotten out of control? I, and I alone, was responsible for that great feat. Why, cats might even call me a hero . . . and make me famous!

The principal turned to face my family, all four of us. "Jesse . . ." He cleared his throat. "Jesse, please take your pets home RIGHT NOW."

I couldn't help myself. I was so happy

that I howled loudly enough to fill the room with sound. Jesse gaped at me. So did his mom. In fact, the whole gang of children looked at me as I danced across Jesse's shoulders. Even the principal and the pig stared.

I meowed at the top of my lungs, "I get to go hooooome!"

TALE'S ENDING

"Another adventure is over. . . ."

from *AdventureCat's*
School Song

I marched back and forth across the top of the car seat and meowed all the way home. The pig snorted and squealed. The instant we got inside the front door, I wrapped myself around Jesse's legs. He fed me a whole can of tuna.

After that, I prowled through the house, checking all the mouse holes. I cleaned myself at the window just like a proper queen. I even let Anna stroke my back once. After all, if she got a teacher like

Ms. Wells, she had a small chance of growing up right.

Then I settled in for the evening on Jesse's lap. He might not be adventurous, but he sure was cuddly. I had decided that cuddling could be important . . . even for an independent cat. Jesse sneaked me bites of his pizza. I got licks of frosting from his birthday cake.

Jesse's mom didn't seem to be kicking him out of the nest, after all. Maybe humans got to live with their mothers forever.

I pounced on the ribbons. I danced across the crinkly paper. Then I curled up in an empty box by Jesse's feet, purring.

I wished the singing cook could be here! I wanted Hopper, the rabbit, to live with me forever. And I wanted Ms. Wells to come visit, too. Friends sure came in all shapes and sizes . . . furry and fur-less, four-legged and two-legged.

I'd caused a marvelous ruckus at school. I'd had a fine adventure, filled with enough excitement to last me for a long, long time! Now I knew exactly where Jesse would be going every morning. Luckily Mrs. White-*dog* didn't expect a boy to catch mice, so she wouldn't starve him.

I cleaned one paw. I needed to remember every detail of my grand adventure so I could tell my own kittens someday. Why, I'd tell them all about the dozens of mice I'd caught at school. I'd tell my kittens how I'd made friends with a wild hopping creature, and how I'd acted like a bobcat. I'd tell them how I'd become an important, famous mascot, and how I was sure the school had built a statue of me after I left.

I yawned at Jesse. Too bad he had to go to school every day to play games. If children were born as brilliant as cats, they wouldn't have to go there so much. Still, he was my human, and I loved him.

I tucked my paws under me and wrapped my tail around as far as it would reach. The crooked tip of my tail covered my nose now! I must have grown up at school!

I purred loudly enough to shake the box.

Cat Whiskers! Bird Feathers! And Mouse Tails!

I, the AdventureCat, was glad to be home again.